Make Your Own Magic

You Choose the Ending!

Starswirl Do-Over

HASBRO and its logo, MY LITTLE PONY, EQUESTRIA GIRLS and all related characters are trademarks of Hasbro and are used with permission. © 2019 Hasbro. All Rights Reserved.

Cover design by Véronique Lefèvre Sweet.

Little, Brown and Company
Hachette Book Group
1290 Avenue of the Americas, New York, NY 10104
Visit us at LBYR.com
MLPEG.com

First Edition: February 2019

Little, Brown and Company is a division of Hachette Book Group, Inc.
The Little, Brown name and logo are trademarks of Hachette Book Group, Inc.

The publisher is not responsible for websites (or their content)
that are not owned by the publisher.

Library of Congress Control Number 2018951544

ISBNs: 978-0-316-41910-9 (pbk.), 978-0-316-41911-6 (ebook)

Printed in the United States of America

LSC-C

10 9 8 7 6 5 4 3 2 1

Make Your Own Magic

You Choose the Ending!

Starswirl Do-Over

Whitney Ralls

Little, Brown and Company

NEW YORK ★ BOSTON

"**S**TARSWIRL MUSIC FESTIVAL, WE HAVE ARRIVED!"

Pinkie Pie's face is pressed against the window of Rarity's sparkling glamping RV, looking out at the colorful sea of tents—the festival campground. Laughing, Sunset Shimmer peels Pinkie's face off the window with a suction sound. Sunset beams. "Just think, Pinkie, in a few short hours we'll be front row for—"

"PostCrush, we know!" Applejack finishes Sunset's sentence for her. "Y'all haven't stopped talking about them the whole way here."

Sunset and Pinkie roll their eyes in unison. "Well, they're only the greatest pop-rock dance duo in recent-memory-slash-history and this is their *huge* reunion show, so *yeah*, we're gonna be talking about 'em!" Sunset elaborates the way only a superfan can. "Kiwi Lollipop, also known as K-Lo, is the cool one. Her favorite color is holographic purple. Favorite hobby: collecting enamel pins."

Pinkie continues, "And Supernova Zap, aka Su-Z, is the zany one! Favorite color: polka dots. Favorite hobby: long walks on the dark side of the moon."

Sunset nods. "Name a more iconic duo—I'll wait!"

Rainbow Dash, Fluttershy, Applejack, and Twilight Sparkle just stare at them.

From the driver's seat, Rarity pipes up. "Iconic duos? Ruching and draping. Sequins and satin. An old classic with a modern twist. The list goes on! But I'll spare you the details because"—the RV lurches to a halt—"it's time to set up camp!"

Night has fallen, and the atmosphere at the campground is electric. Distant laughter and thumping bass lines float on the air with the scents of fried food and the surrounding trees. At a neighboring campsite, Zephyr Breeze sets up a slackline between two trees and takes a few wobbly steps across it. The Mane Seven huddle around a campfire, toasting marshmallows.

"What are you guys most excited to do at the festival?" Twilight asks brightly. Without missing a beat, Rainbow Dash and Applejack cover Sunset's and Pinkie's mouths, muffling them. "We know what you guys are looking forward to most."

Applejack tosses her hat onto a nearby stump. "I'm fixin' to win some carnival games. There's a giant stuffed animal with my name on it in there." She shoots a competitive glance toward Sunset. "Bet you a front-row seat at PostCrush you can't beat me."

Rainbow Dash scoffs. "Carnival games? This is a *music* festival, my friend. It's about the bands! Deviant Septum is playing, and their guitarist is the fastest on record! Of course, I've personally never been timed, so who's to say I'm not faster?"

"Tut-tut!" Rarity chimes in. "What is a festival without fashion? Vintage markets with every poncho, parasol, and platform shoe you could want!"

Twilight Sparkle adds, "Don't forget the art installations and food trucks and rides—"

Sunset can't hold it back, bursting out, "And PostCrush!"

"Yes, and PostCrush." Twilight sighs. "But before then, we've got to get a good night's sleep!"

Inside the glamping RV, Sunset's snuggled

into her ultra-plush bunk, drif

sleep. Pinkie sticks her head dc

bunk above. "I'm too excited to

Sunset smacks her lips, barel

try, Pinkie. In the morning, we're gonna start the most perfect day ever."

Pinkie nods, going back into her bunk. A second later, "Is it morning yet?"

"No."

"How 'bout now? Or now?"

"No and no."

"'Kay, but it's definitely morning now, right?"

In unison, the rest of the Mane Seven sound out from the dark: *"GO TO SLEEP, PINKIE!"*

A few hours later, Sunset's eyes blearily open to see Pinkie Pie's eyes an inch away. *"IT'S MORNING!"*

Yeah, I noticed." Sunset laughs.

Rarity twirls, showing off her beaded poncho. "I've finally decided on my Starswirl day-one look! Or, wait, should I switch out the wide-brimmed hat for a flower crown? So many festival-ready ensembles, but so little time!"

Meanwhile, Pinkie Pie is talking a mile a minute. "I can't believe Starswirl day one is already so much fun, even before we're inside the festival. Starswirl morning one for the win!"

Later, under the watchful eye of a serious security guard, the Mane Seven scan their wristbands and head into the festival. *Beep! Beep! Beep!* They're in!

The spectacular wonderland of Starswirl unfolds before them. A giant Star Swirl the Bearded balloon, friends laughing and waving giant inflatable flowers—even a girl on stilts! The Mane Seven's mouths hang agape.

"What surprises lie ahead?" Pinkie wonders out loud.

POOF! A confetti cannon bursts forth, sprinkling them with joy.

"THERE'S A CONFETTI CANNON?!" Pinkie shrieks.

Sunset wipes the paper from her eyes, determined. "In just a few short hours, I'll actually be in the presence of K-Lo and Su-Z, breathing the same air, under the same stars!"

Pinkie nods. "But until then...the fun of Starswirl day one! What do you wanna do first, Sunset?"

Sunset furrows her brow. What *should* she do first? As Rarity would say, there are so many activities, but so little time! Sunset spots some promising art installations nearby, but then a bar overflowing with ice cream and human-size toppings catches her eye. Not to mention that PostCrush has a meet and greet scheduled for this afternoon.

You decide what Sunset does!

➡ To check out the festival's art installations, **GO TO PAGE 9**.

➡ To investigate the giant ice-cream bar, **GO TO PAGE 14**.

➡ To get PostCrush's autographs, **GO TO PAGE 18**.

SUNSET SHIMMER LEADS PINKIE PIE
TOWARD THE ART INSTALLATIONS....

The giant balloon of Star Swirl the Bearded
looms overhead, tethered to the ground by a
big rope in the midst of the art.

"These installations were specially commis-
sioned for the Starswirl festival! Why not get a
well-rounded dose of culture while we're here?"
Sunset stops to look at an intricate web of
brightly colored strings. She nods, appreciat-
ing it. Pinkie Pie rises up behind her shoulder,
squinting.

"But what does it mean?" Pinkie asks.

Sunset considers. "Art is about whatever
it makes you feel. This makes me feel as if
we're all connected." Pinkie's perturbed, trying
to see it from different angles. Sunset moves

on to futuristic neon goggles that sit on a pedestal.

"Care to try the Starswirl virtual-reality experience?" a festival worker asks.

"Um, only definitely!"

Sunset pulls on the goggles, and suddenly—

"I'm flying over Starswirl!" She spreads her arms. "This is amazing and also kind of dizzying! Pinkie, you gotta try this!"

Nearby, Pinkie is assessing a stack of pink and green boxes. "Hold on, Sunset, I think I'm getting the hang of this whole art thing." Her eyes narrow. "*Hmm*, yes. When you don't believe in yourself, you put yourself in a box." She wipes away a tear, and then...another festival worker clears away the boxes. They were just boxes, not art!

Pinkie coughs and moves along. "I mean, nothing, I knew that wasn't art!" In her rush, she trips over the rope tethering the Star Swirl balloon to the ground. It hooks Pinkie's ankle and pulls her into the air. Panicking, Pinkie waggles her arms for help. She grabs Sunset Shimmer, who's still in virtual-reality land.

"This is amazing! If I didn't know any better, I'd swear I was really, really...really...Is that a breeze?" Sunset lifts her goggles. "*FLYING! Pinkie, what happened?!*"

"*ALL I WANTED TO DO WAS APPRECIATE ART!*" Pinkie wails. Then she takes a look around. "Hey, at least the view's pretty good from up here."

Sunset also looks down—she's got a point! "There's the main stage!" But the balloon floats right over it. "And there it goes. Along with our chance of seeing PostCrush."

Pinkie gulps. "Look at the bright side. At least we've got a good view of...the trees." Sunset groans, but Pinkie doubles down.

"Honestly, I feel bad for our friends back at Starswirl, missing out on all these trees. What are they doing? Seeing cool bands, eating spicy-melon shaved ice, making memories to last a lifetime—boring! I'll take the trees, thank you very much. Right, Sunset? Oh look, an actual sunset!"

Sunset's boiling. She lets out a scream that echoes through the forest.

It's nighttime when the balloon finally descends, popping against a treetop. The distant roar of a crowd and music is drowned out by the whooshing air blowing out of the balloon, right into Sunset's face as she struggles to untangle herself from the ropes. Pinkie giggles nervously. "Well, not quite a perfect night."

"Not perfect? You totally ruined it! Post-Crush is playing *right* now, and we're not going to get to see them! I wish I could do this day over again." Sunset huffs as she trudges off into the woods, back toward the campground.

Pinkie Pie runs to catch up with her. "I wish we could do it over again, too."

Sunset shakes her head. "Not *we*. *Me*. As in, if I could do this day over, I'd do it *without* you."

At a loss, Pinkie slows down. Sunset walks ahead. "I guess I'll see you back at the RV, then?"

Sunset shrugs. "Whatever."

Sunset looks over her shoulder, a little guilty, but shakes it off and keeps walking, muttering to herself, "All I wanted was one perfect day."

She doesn't see it, but a pulse of purple energy ripples past her. When she finally reaches the RV, she looks back at the trees and sighs, "Tomorrow's a new day."

➡ **GO TO PAGE 24.**

"*Ummm*, **MOUNTAINS OF ICE CREAM AND MASSIVE TOPPINGS? SAY NO MORE.**"

Sunset Shimmer struggles with a waist-high ice-cream cone. "I have a feeling we can share one, Pinkie! Want to choose toppings?" Pinkie Pie gawks at a gummy pony the size of her head. Her eyes are as wide as saucers. Sunset waves in front of her eyes. "Uh, Pinkie? Are you here?" Sunset bites her lip, realizing she's created a monster. "Uh-oh."

"T-t-toppings?" Pinkie's trancelike state turns into a quaking hyperactivity. "Toppings!"

Pinkie Pie swan-dives into a swimming pool full of sprinkles. A festival worker leans over sheepishly. "Excuse me, miss, but those are food-grade and swimming in them isn't up to health code."

"You can't stop me from living my dreams!"

Sunset face-palms. "This can't be good."

Sunset chases Pinkie Pie under a chocolate waterfall, across some lollipop lily pads, and finally corners her at a picket fence of Popsicle sticks. Sunset tries to reason with her. "Pinkie, step away from the cotton candy."

Pinkie's eyes are wide—she's got sugar fever. "I could spend all day here, Sunset!"

Sunset checks her watch—it's getting late! "We already have, Pinkie! PostCrush is about to go onstage. We gotta run!"

"So let's run!" Pinkie bolts off, and Sunset tries to follow—but she can't move! Her feet are stuck in a caramel river. She pulls off her boots and chases after Pinkie, who ducks into a nearby tent. Sunset hears her exclaim, "Giant ice-cream sandwiches?! My life is complete!"

Sunset rolls her eyes and dives into the tent—colliding with Pinkie!

"Come on, Pinkie. Let's—*mmph*!"

SPLURCH! Two cookies collide with ice cream, and the next thing Sunset and Pinkie know, they're stuck together in the middle of a giant ice-cream sandwich. Sunset is resilient, trying to soldier on.

"Come on, we can still make it to Post-Crush!" But she waddles a few steps, and the two fall over flat. Pinkie happily nibbles at the ice cream.

Sunset sighs. "We're not making it to Post-Crush, are we?"

Later, at the glamping RV, Sunset glumly washes the goopy melted ice cream out of her hair. Pinkie's still licking her fingers. "At least tomorrow's a new day. We can still have fun at Starswirl."

"Seriously, Pinkie? I had one chance to see PostCrush, and you blew it for me. Today was supposed to be perfect."

"But we still had fun, right?" Pinkie offers. Sunset looks away, irritated.

"I think I'm gonna take a walk and clear my head."

Pinkie sinks as she watches Sunset go.

In the woods, Sunset looks sadly over her shoulder at the RV. She hears laughter. "I wish I could do this day over again. *Without* her." She doesn't see it, but a pulse of purple energy ripples past her....

➡ **GO TO PAGE 24.**

THE LINE TO GET POSTCRUSH'S AUTOGRAPHS WRAPS AROUND THE FESTIVAL.

"But it's gonna be so totally worth it!" Sunset Shimmer is brimming with excitement, clutching a limited-edition PostCrush tee for them to sign. She takes a slurp of her extra-large frozen lemonade. The rest of the Mane Seven wait with her, a little less eager.

Fluttershy cranes her neck. "We sure could use a bird's-eye view. I can't even see the front of the line!"

Rainbow Dash cracks her knuckles. "No way to make it move faster, but I can move fast to figure out how close we are!" With that, she zooms down the line and out of sight.

Rarity chimes in. "Not to worry, darlings,

we can simply pass the time by helping me choose accessories for my festival season lookbook!" She tries on different sunglasses. "What do you think of these, Sunset?"

Sunset starts to speak, but before she can, Rarity answers, "Too square. Too round. Too dark. Not dark enough." Rarity builds to full panic, trying them on at lightning speed. "Wrong. Wrong. Wrong. Wrong. Wrong!" She gulps. "I'm going to need more sunglasses. Sorry, Sunset—got to run to the vintage market."

"That's o—"

"Thanks for understanding. *Byeee!*" Rarity's already gone.

"—kay," finishes Sunset. She takes a slurp of lemonade.

Rainbow Dash zips up, out of breath. "Listen, I'm not saying this line is long, I'm saying this line is super, super, extra bonkers long. I'd normally be totally down to wait patiently with you guys, but...I'm gonna catch a show instead!" With a quick wave, Rainbow Dash jets off again.

Fluttershy looks down shyly. "A little birdie told me that she doesn't actually want to wait in line." Suddenly, a little birdie really does fly by, tweeting a song. Fluttershy's eyes go wide. "In fact, that little birdie told me it needs help gathering materials for its nest! I'll see you later, Sunset!" Fluttershy hurries after the bird.

Applejack gives Sunset a quick hug. "And I gotta run and wrangle some rope for the rodeo contest."

Sunset takes a sip of her lemonade and looks to Twilight Sparkle and Pinkie Pie. "Well, at least the three of us are seizing the once-in-a-lifetime opportunity to meet PostCrush."

Twilight checks her watch. "Actually, if my calculations are correct, I have to leave now if I'm going to see the lecture on space-time."

"There's a lecture on space-time at Starswirl Music Festival?"

"No, it's online!"

Sunset sighs as Twilight Sparkle runs off, too. She turns to Pinkie, who gives her a thumbs-up. "Looks as if it's just you and me!" Sunset slurps the lemonade dry but then realizes she has to use the bathroom! She asks Pinkie to hold their place in line.

But when Sunset returns, Pinkie is gone! She turns around to see Pinkie walking up with two berry-swirled churros.

"Pinkie! I thought you were waiting in line for us!"

"I was! Except it was the food-truck line!"

Sunset is furious—now they'll never get to the front of the line to meet PostCrush! The meet and greet is ending! But Pinkie thinks on her feet.

"Excuse me, mister?" Pinkie Pie taps on the

shoulder of a guy working at Puffed Pastry's famous dessert food truck. "Can we borrow your delivery cart? It's a pastry emergency!" He nods, and soon Sunset and Pinkie are speeding in the delivery golf cart, chasing down Post-Crush's VIP golf cart! Sunset can see K-Lo and Su-Z just a few feet ahead! Pinkie pumps the gas.

"Almost...there!"

"Pinkie, watch out!"

The golf cart speeds right into the Star Swirl the Bearded parade balloon. They bounce off and into a jumble. PostCrush's VIP cart slows down just long enough for Sunset to see K-Lo shoot her some major side-eye. Then it whizzes off!

Sunset's distraught. "Could this day get any worse?!"

Just then, the security guard grabs them by their collars. "Destruction of property, fabrication of a pastry emergency...You two are hereby banned from Starswirl."

Back at the glamping RV, Sunset is not a happy glamper. She sulks by the fire while Pinkie roasts marshmallows. "If it weren't for you, we would've met PostCrush, *and* we'd be front row at their concert right now."

Pinkie tries to cheer her up, throwing a marshmallow. It explodes into confetti. "Look, a shooting star! Make a wish!"

Sunset turns away. "If I made a wish, it would be to do this day over again. *Without* you."

Sunset takes one look at Pinkie's hurt face and walks away from the RV and into the woods and looks up at the sky. Not a shooting star in sight. She sighs, closing her eyes, and doesn't notice the wisps of purple magic that ripple past her.

➡ GO TO PAGE 24.

THE NEXT MORNING...

Sunset Shimmer tosses and turns, grumbling in her sleep. Her eyes slowly blink open to see Pinkie Pie's eyes an inch away.

"IT'S MORNING!"

"Pinkie, quit it. Are you going to wake me up like that every morning?" Sunset groans, covering her head with a pillow.

"I've finally decided on my Starswirl day-one look!" Rarity declares. "Or, wait, should I switch out the wide-brimmed hat for a flower crown? So many festival-ready ensembles, but so little time!"

"I can't believe Starswirl day one is already so much fun, even before we're inside the festival. Starswirl morning one for the win!" Pinkie cheers.

Sunset's eyes shoot open.

"Did you say Starswirl day *one*?"

"Why, yes, dear. Why? Do you think it's too gauche? I can change! I don't want to start off the festival on the wrong foot, in the wrong shoe!"

Sunset's confused. Something must be wrong.

She'd already gone through the trauma that was Starswirl day one. How can this be happening?

Then it dawns on her.

"My wish!"

The rest of the Mane Seven look at her.

"You made a wish?" Fluttershy asks.

"What kinda wish are we talking about here?" Rainbow Dash demands.

"WHY DIDN'T YOU TELL ME WE WERE WISHING WISHES?!" Pinkie explodes.

Sunset turns away, still processing. The day is repeating!

What should Sunset do?

➡ Have the perfect do-over! Her wish came true! Now she has the chance to do just what she wants and see PostCrush. **GO TO PAGE 27**.

➡ Ask her friends for help. Whatever's going on here, she can't face it alone. **GO TO PAGE 56**.

➡ Go back to sleep. This is definitely a dream. **GO TO PAGE 87**.

SUNSET SHIMMER GOT HER WISH!

And she's not about to waste it.

Inside the festival, Sunset rushes past all the distractions. Giant ice-cream bar? Pass. Art installations? No way. PostCrush's meet and greet? Better not risk it. This time, she's gonna be in the audience for PostCrush front and center, even if it means spending hours waiting at the stage.

A food-truck worker calls out to her, tempting her with free samples of deep-fried candy bars. A lounge's neon lights beckon. At the vintage market, unique beaded necklaces jangle in the breeze. Without blinking, Sunset runs right past it all.

Pinkie Pie runs, panting, trying to keep up with her.

"Sunset, where are you going, and why are you going so fast?! *OOF!*" Pinkie hits the guard-rail where Sunset plants her hand, triumphant.

"Front and center."

"But PostCrush doesn't play for hours! We should have a festival adventure until then!" Pinkie Pie pulls out a festival map. "Like here, here, here, here, or over here!"

"Thanks, but I did my adventuring yesterday."

Pinkie Pie squints, trying to do the math on that. "You mean, on the way to Starswirl?"

Sunset just waves her off. "You go have fun—I'm staying right here."

Pinkie's surprised and disappointed, hanging her head.

"Oh okay. I thought we were gonna do it together."

"It's my festival, too, and this is how I want to spend it."

Pinkie nods and heads out, crestfallen.

Sunset keeps her hand on the rail, front and center, stone-faced, as different acts take the stage. A country pop singer drawls, a DJ duo wicky-wicks, a hip-hop crew hypes, but none of them get a smile from Sunset. She's on a mission.

As dusk falls, Sunset is drooping at the guardrail, half-asleep. Someone nudges her, and she perks up. "Pinkie Pie?"

But it's a stranger. In fact, fans are packed like sardines all around her, but she has the best seat in the house. At last, she smiles.

"This—"

The lights go down.

"Is—"

The first note echoes.

"Perfect!"

As the lights come up from the corners of the stage, the crowd goes wild. PostCrush stands in silhouette for a tense, exciting moment— and then they launch into their hit song.

Sunset is in awe as K-Lo wails on her electric guitar. "So cool!" Sunset looks to her left and right, expecting Pinkie Pie to be there. But she's not. Sunset shakes it off. No reason for her not to have fun.

Colored projections flash, K-Lo and Su-Z dance-battle in between songs, and Sunset loses her voice from screaming so much. K-Lo finishes an unreal guitar solo, then tosses her pick into the crowd.

Sunset jumps...

...and catches it!

After the most incredible show of her whole life, Sunset walks back to the glamping RV, running her finger along the guitar pick. What a perfect day.

"Okay, Universe, you really came through on this one. I promise I'll never ask for anything ever again!" she says, looking out at the stars.

The next morning, Sunset smiles, rolling over in her sleep.

"IT'S MORNING!" Pinkie Pie shrieks. Sunset opens her eyes, skeptical. She looks around. There's Pinkie, hovering inches above her, and Rarity twirling in front of the mirror in her beaded poncho. Oh *no*. It's the same morning all over again! Her eyes widen.

"Umm, Universe, can we have a word?"

Sunset thought fulfilling her wish would solve this whole repeating-day situation, but clearly it's a little more complex than that.

What should Sunset do?

➡ Ask her friends for help. This is too big to handle by herself. **GO TO PAGE 56**.

➡ Take advantage of the situation. More time at one of the coolest festivals around? Yes, please! **GO TO PAGE 67**.

SUNSET SHIMMER DUCKS RIGHT.

Rarity follows her as she barrels down the pathway.

"I'm pretty sure she ran this way!" Sunset shouts.

The garden walls curve overhead, and they suddenly find themselves in a tunnel. It is lit only by the neon lights running along either side of them. The tunnel is seemingly endless, and the farther they go, the more the neon lights twist into a swirling pattern.

They run, but it's as if they're not going forward.

"Are we even moving?" Sunset asks, frustrated.

"Never mind that, darling. This color palette is driving me absolutely mad! Neon purple with neon lime? Whose sick idea of fun is this? Why is this happening to me?!"

Rarity drops to her knees, clutching her head. Who knew a color scheme could affect a person so much? Sunset shifts objectives. Forget finding that mysterious stranger—Sunset has to get Rarity out of here before she has a full-blown meltdown.

Sunset hoists up Rarity and runs back in the direction they came. Except the colors keep swirling. The tunnel doesn't end. It's as if the entrance has vanished! Sunset slows to a halt. Rarity's laughing now, shouting, "LIME AND PURPLE AND LIME AND PURPLE!"

Sunset sighs. So much for that. It's going to be a long night.

➡ GO TO PAGE 102.

"EVERY DAY IS THE SAME, OVER AND OVER AGAIN..."

"Okay, those lyrics can't be a coincidence." Sunset Shimmer is sure whoever's singing those words must be the culprit behind her current predicament.

With her friends, Sunset tears across the festival grounds toward a secondary stage, where a significant crowd has gathered. Sunset jumps, not quite able to see through the crowd.

Silver Spoon and Diamond Tiara sing along:

"Again and again,
when will it end?
We're stuck here with all these
humans for friends."

"Excuse me, what band is playing?" Flutter-shy asks. But everyone's swept up in the song, singing along as if entranced. Twilight Sparkle checks her festival schedule as Sunset pushes through the crowd. She gasps.

"The Dazzlings are playing Starswirl!" Twilight announces, horrified.

Sunset looks up as Adagio Dazzle, Sonata Dusk, and Aria Blaze sing their auto-tuned song onstage.

Sunset is furious. "Can't they leave us alone?! They must be back to their old tricks, using Equestrian magic to regain their voices and control the masses with music!"

Pinkie Pie starts pushing through the crowd, rolling up her sleeves. "Lemme at 'em! Things are about to get seriously serious!" Pinkie grabs at her forearm again, meeting skin, and pauses. "I wish I had more sleeves to roll up!"

"What are you going to do?" Twilight Sparkle asks, grabbing Pinkie's and Sunset's shoulders. "Just jump onstage?"

"Yes!" Sunset cries.

Rainbow Dash points out the security guard standing next to the stage. "Or we could go backstage and take 'em on." Rainbow Dash pulls out some sunglasses seemingly from nowhere and puts them on.

"But we're not VIP," Fluttershy points out. "I mean, you're Very Important People to me, but we aren't to them. How will you get past the security guard?"

"We'll just sneak past him," Rainbow Dash says with a shrug.

"No!" Applejack says. "What we gotta do is march up to this guy and tell him we mean business!"

Sunset considers.

What should Sunset do?

➡ Jump onstage and confront the Dazzlings. **GO TO PAGE 99**.

➡ Find a way backstage. **GO TO PAGE 129**.

THE WHO'S WHO OF STARSWIRL
LOUNGE BACKSTAGE.

Shimmery lights, picture-perfect snacks,
custom infused sodas. It's as if there's a beauti-
ful, sparkly Snapgab filter over everything and
everyone. Sunset Shimmer's in awe as she
passes the familiar faces of up-and-coming
artists. There's mastermind producer Peony
Petunia talking to country troubadour Dirk
Thistleweed. Oh, and that's DJ Pon-3 swap-
ping singles with techno-pop vocalist MC Dex
Effex! And that's...

That's...

"PostCrush!" Her voice cracks as she says it
aloud, and Peony Petunia side-eyes her. K-Lo
lounges on a chaise, looking at her phone,
while Su-Z sways, spacing out on a swing set.

Yes, they literally have a swing set in the artists' lounge. Sunset shakes it off, trying to play it cool.

Just then, the Dazzlings walk in and collapse on furry, glittery beanbag chairs.

What should Sunset do?

➡ Confront the Dazzlings.
GO TO PAGE 52.

➡ Meet PostCrush. **GO TO PAGE 96.**

SHE MAY BE CAUGHT IN A TIME LOOP, BUT SUNSET SHIMMER DOESN'T HAVE TIME TO MESS AROUND.

Twilight Sparkle explains it to Sunset. They know that the reset point happens sometime between going to sleep and waking up. All Sunset has to do to break the time part of this space-time kerfuffle is pull an all-nighter.

"And lucky for you, I've pulled a few in my time," Twilight says as she cockily polishes her glasses. "Not for studying, of course. Sometimes I just can't put down the book I'm reading!"

"So what will happen once I stay awake through the reset point?"

"That's the fun of an experiment—we don't know!"

Sunset slowly raises a skeptical eyebrow.

Twilight Sparkle clears her throat. "Theoretically, you'll escape the time loop and stay awake into the next day of Starswirl."

Sunset's eyes glimmer with hope. "Sleepovers are always the most fun when you don't get much sleeping done."

Twilight agrees. "Now, first things first— coffee!"

Twilight and Sunset find a gourmet coffee cart. They slurp mochas, gulp down chai lattes, and munch on coffee beans. As they work their way through the menu, Sunset can't help thinking that she's never wanted a day to pass so quickly. It's like the last day of school before summer vacation. Except *this is* supposed to be the vacation! She looks at the time. It's only two o'clock? She yawns.

HOOOOOONK!

Twilight Sparkle blasts an air horn. "No yawning allowed. If we're going to stay awake all night, we're going to need to keep our adrenaline up. Luckily, Starswirl has lots of energizing activities. But first, cappuccino."

Sunset wears virtual-reality goggles, feeling as if she's soaring through the air.

"Woaaaah!" She waggles her arms, trying to keep her balance, spilling her cold brew.

Twilight giggles until the booth attendant puts goggles on her. "WAHHHH!"

Later, Sunset and Twilight Sparkle lick cones of coffee ice cream and walk past a paint party. *SPLAT!* Sunset's suddenly hit with a water balloon filled with pink paint. Bulk Biceps is the culprit. She looks to Twilight, and in unison, they shrug, smiling. Together they hurl their cones at him—*SPLURCH!* With that, they dive into the paint party, laughing as they smear blue, orange, and purple across canvases and launch yellow paint cannonballs across the field. They're a multicolored mess, and Sunset's invigorated. All this excitement is definitely going to keep her awake!

But soon enough, Sunset is snoozing into a coffee-flavored cinnamon bun.

"Wake up, we've got a hypothesis to prove!" Twilight lifts Sunset's closed eyelid.

Sunset groans. "Not exactly thrilling."

Twilight Sparkle considers. "If you need a thrill, maybe it's time we go full sleepover mode." She gets a dangerous glint in her eye. "Truth. Or. Dare."

Sunset sits bolt upright. "Are you serious?"

"Dare it is."

"Wait, no—I didn't—!"

"Find the cutest guy at Starswirl and ask him out."

"Twilight, if your hypothesis does break the time loop, I'll really be asking him out!"

"In that case, I double-dare you."

Sunset gulps. Then she sees him.

His perfectly tousled hair would make Flash Sentry envious. Rarity would nod in approval of his trendy but understated denim jacket. As he walks by, Snips and Snails literally fall all over each other, bowled over by his effortless coolness. And, with even more coolness, he helps them to their feet.

"Easy there, guys. Save some for the bumper cars."

Snips and Snails laugh, charmed. All that, *and* he's funny?

He walks past Sunset, giving her a shy smile. Twilight Sparkle nudges her. "You got this. Just be cool, calm, and—"

"HEY, DO YOU WANNA GO OUT SOMETIME?!"

Sunset jumps to her feet, awkwardly drawing the attention of what feels like everyone at Starswirl. Including the coolest guy she's ever seen. He stares at her, caught off guard. Sunset panics, thinking of how she can play it off, when he smiles.

"Yeah, how about right now?"

No doubt about it: Sunset's adrenaline is officially pumping.

Long after the sun's gone down, Sunset's worries about the time loop are far behind her. She and the boy are laughing, sharing stories and a basket of French fries. Sunset's cheeks hurt from smiling so much. They have so much in common! They both are secretly afraid of scary movies. Sunset loves to draw comics, and he loves to paint watercolors. Sure, Sunset is a pony from Equestria transformed into a human, but they both think ketchup is overrated! Plus, he is so cute when he grins at her and says, "I'm really glad you asked me out. Not a lot of girls would do that."

She shrugs. "I'm glad I did, too. I wouldn't have done it normally, but there were special circumstances."

"You're right, I'd say this is a pretty special circumstance," he says a little bashfully. He leans in to kiss her, and she closes her eyes, leaning in as well.

WHOOSH.

Sunset opens her eyes, and she's suddenly sitting alone in the library of Canterlot High School. What?!

Twilight Sparkle, Rainbow Dash, and Pinkie Pie enter the library, abuzz with excitement.

"Starswirl tickets go on sale in five minutes!" Twilight announces.

"I sure hope we get 'em!" adds Applejack.

"Sunset, can you believe we might get to see PostCrush?!" Pinkie Pie can hardly contain herself. But Sunset's mind is miles away, back at Starswirl.

She looks around wildly. "What just happened? Where did he go?!"

Pinkie Pie cocks her head, confused. "Where did who go?"

Sunset's at a loss. She didn't even get his name.... It all felt so real, but could everything that happened just have been a dream? Or did breaking the time loop create some kind of reverse time slingshot?

"I got the tickets!"

The other girls cheer while Sunset smiles thoughtfully. She'll just have to keep an eye out for a watercolor-painting, scary-movie-fearing cutie in a denim jacket.

THE END

SAGE SMOKE WAFTS. A WIND CHIME SWAYS IN THE BREEZE.

Sunset Shimmer stands in the middle of the yoga yurt, in a perfect tree pose. After weeks of back-to-back yoga, the student has become the master. Sandalwood watches in awe as Sunset does flawless sun salutations.

"They're...perfect."

Without opening her eyes, Sunset calmly replies, "Even if my execution were imperfect, I would no less be happy with them. They are exactly how they need to be."

Sandalwood's eyes go even wider. "So wise... I didn't know you were into yoga, Sunset... Sunset?"

But Sunset is now cross-legged on the floor, meditating serenely. Her mind is blank. She is completely present, in harmony with the universe. She blinks her eyes. How long has passed? Minutes? Hours? She can't tell, and truthfully, it does not matter.

But now that her eyes are open, she can clearly see that Sandalwood has a crush on her.

"Sunset, I have a crush on you."

Sunset pats his head kindly and shares her infinite wisdom. "Crushes do not matter. This moment, like this crush, is fleeting and no different than the next."

Sandalwood nods, soaking this in.

"Time has no beginning nor end," Sunset continues, "and therefore my need to 'escape' the time loop is no longer relevant."

Sandalwood squints, really trying to follow. He plays it cool and nods. "I totally get it."

The faintest hint of concern begins to reach Sunset's super-calm face. "Yep. I totally don't care about breaking the time loop at all. At... all."

Mid-meditation, Sunset's eye twitches. Uh-oh.

Maybe enlightenment isn't all it's cracked up to be. Maybe she should just...get away.

⟹ **GO TO PAGE 82.**

"**R**AINBOW DASH IS RIGHT."

"*Ummm*, obviously," Rainbow Dash says with a flip of her multicolored hair. "Wait, what am I right about?"

Sunset Shimmer explains: As long as she's stuck in this time loop, she might as well have some fun! It'll probably work itself out. In the meantime, the festival is hers to explore! But Starswirl has so much to offer. Where to start?

What should Sunset do?

➡ Relax to the max in the yoga yurts.
GO TO PAGE 69.

➡ Have a fashion show. **GO TO PAGE 93**.

➡ See. Every. Single. Band. **GO TO PAGE 135**.

"THE LOOP IS TOTALLY WORKING!"

Sunset Shimmer would know Sonata Dusk's grating, untrustworthy voice anywhere.

"Of course it is, it was my idea," seethes Adagio Dazzle.

Sunset grits her teeth. So they *are* the ones behind the time loop. Well, Sunset's not about to let them get away with it. She marches over and takes the mini-calzone right out of Aria Blaze's hand. She eats it in one bite.

"Hey, I'm hungry!" Aria protests.

"What exactly are you doing here?" Adagio asks pointedly.

"The same thing you are," Sunset snaps back. "Living the same day over and over again. Admit it—you're the ones who caused the time loop!"

They stare at her blankly.

"Unsurprisingly, she has no idea what she's talking about." Adagio sighs.

Aria laughs derisively. "A time loop? As if!"

At this point, Sunset's interruption starts to draw stares from the ultra-chic musicians around her. Could she be wrong?

She clears her throat and asks a little quieter, "Then what was that loop you were talking about?"

"A *vocal* loop. Duh. Pretty basic songwriting stuff but probably *way* too advanced for the Rainbooms." Sonata smirks.

"But...the lyrics to your song. *Every day is the same, over and over again*? I thought you were the ones causing Starswirl day one to repeat over and over again!"

"Nope, that song's about being stuck in this wretched human world day after day," Aria hisses.

"Besides, why would we want to keep living the same day over and over?" Adagio scoffs.

Sunset thinks.

"This all started when I wanted to have a perfect day. And when Pinkie Pie ruined it the first time around, I wished I could have a redo. I'm sure performing at such a big music festival would put even more pressure on you to have a perfect performance."

Sunset expects the worst from Adagio. But instead, Adagio puts a hand on her shoulder and smiles.

"Nothing's ever perfect. It's the mistakes and the choices we make with our friends that make our life, well...not perfect, but *ours*. When we perform as the Dazzlings now, it's real. It's us. Because we do it without the help of magic."

"Unless of course, you count the magic of auto-tune," Sonata chirps.

"Which I don't," Adagio snips icily.

Sunset feels Adagio's words echo in her chest. She has been blaming Pinkie Pie for ruining Starswirl this whole time, when really it was Sunset who ruined the night by getting mad at her. If only she could do that first day over again...

"Wait a minute..."

She can! Sunset runs off, waving to the Dazzlings over her shoulder.

"I never thought I'd say this, but...thanks, Adagio!"

Adagio rolls her eyes.

➡ GO TO PAGE 91.

SUNSET SHIMMER DOESN'T KNOW WHAT'S GOING ON, BUT SHE DOESN'T HAVE TO FIGURE IT OUT ALONE.

Her friends are always there to make things better. Right?

"Yeah, right."

"So you're telling us the day is *repeating*?"

"Are you sure you're feeling all right?"

Sunset puts her head in her hands. "I can't explain it, either, but yes! We've all definitely lived Starswirl day one before, but I'm the only one who remembers it...."

They scan their wristbands to get into the festival.

Twilight Sparkle adjusts her glasses, concerned. "Could it be déjà vu?"

Sunset calmly predicts, "Confetti cannon in three, two, one."

POOF! Right on cue.

Pinkie Pie's elated. "What a cool magic trick!"

"It's not a trick, Pinkie. Something is seriously wrong here."

"It may not be a magic trick, but it has Equestrian magic written all over it. Maybe Princess Twilight Sparkle could help us," Twilight suggests.

Later, in the cool shade of a Starswirl lounging yurt ("Great decor!" Rarity exclaims), Sunset writes in her diary. And sure enough, Princess Twilight Sparkle writes back:

> The day keeps repeating?
> You can say that again. (Sorry,
> couldn't resist!) Unfortunately,
> your situation makes all too much
> sense. An ancient Equestrian relic
> recently went missing, and it must
> have somehow found its way to
> the human realm. The Time

Twirler is a powerful device that allows the user to rewind a day, up to twenty-four hours. Someone at the festival must have it! The only way to break the loop is to press down the Time Twirler's pin, thereby deactivating it.

Sunset sits back, deflated. Now there are even more questions. "But who would do this? And why?"

Twilight leans forward, excited. "Pardon me, but there are even more questions than that! The hypotheses we could test are infinite! Is space-time more linked to space or time? Does the moment of reset have a physical effect on the world? If a person's stuck in the time loop, do they age?" She notices Sunset's weary glare and clams up. "Sorry, I know this is a big problem. But it's a big, exciting, scientifically relevant problem!"

"Problem? More like superpower!" Rainbow Dash throws herself on the ground dramatically. "Starswirl has way more to offer than you can experience in one day. I've been having so much trouble deciding what I want to do. And Sunset has enough time to do it all!"

An echoing giggle catches Sunset's attention. She turns around but is hardly able to catch a glimpse of someone silhouetted in the yurt's doorway. Sunset lunges outside, but the mysterious stranger is already bolting away. Weird.

But what's even weirder is the distant song she hears next:

> *"Every day is the same,*
> *the same, the same.*
> *Over and over again,*
> *again, again..."*

It's coming from a nearby stage!

What should Sunset do?

➡ Follow the suspicious song.
GO TO PAGE 34.

➡ Take advantage of her newfound superpower! **GO TO PAGE 51.**

➡ Use the scientific method with Twilight Sparkle. **GO TO PAGE 77.**

➡ Confront the mysterious stranger.
GO TO PAGE 127.

*S*PLAT!

At the paint party, joyful festivalgoers fling bright pigment at one another in a designated obstacle course. Sunset Shimmer and Pinkie Pie are, of course, on the pink team. They work in perfect unison: a rainbow ballet through the squelching fountains of blue, yellow, and purple.

Bam. They take out Snips and Snails and celebrate, putting pink battle paint under their eyes.

At the human pinball field, Sunset and Pinkie squeeze into a giant inflatable ball. *They* are the pinball! Together, they knock down some giant dominoes, bounce off a wall, and slingshot around the bend. They're racking up the points, bouncing all over the place!

They're bouncing so much in fact that they bounce over the wall! They're rolling across the festival grounds, right for the big crowd at the main stage!

Sunset tries to backtrack. "Uh-oh!"

"Sunset, jump!"

They jump together, and the ball soars into the air! Suddenly, they're being lifted up by the crowd. They're crowd-surfing! It's as if the crowd is batting around a giant beach ball, except *they* are the beach ball! Sunset laughs, having more fun than she has had on any of her days here.

The crowd bounces them right over the security guard's head! They're backstage!

Sunset and Pinkie tumble out of the human pinball, laughing their butts off.

"That was so fun!" Pinkie can hardly breathe she's laughing so hard. Then her stomach growls. "On to the food-truck tasting! I hope the lines aren't too long."

Sunset notices the artists' lounge nearby.

"I'll do you one better."

Inside the artists' lounge, every food truck has a table set up. And the best part? No lines! Pinkie Pie has stars in her eyes and pastries in her mouth.

"This is everything I ever dreamed Starswirl would be!" she says through a mouth full of deep-fried cotton candy.

"And more," agrees Sunset, pointing out none other than PostCrush! They're sitting right behind them! Pinkie Pie's mouth drops open, and Sunset shuts it for her, teasing, "Chew your food! We're about to meet PostCrush!"

➡ GO TO PAGE 112.

SUNSET SHIMMER CAN'T BELIEVE IT—
SHE'S MEETING POSTCRUSH!

Su-Z squeezes the Alicorn plushie in delight, while K-Lo signs an autograph for Sunset.

"I'm a huge fan," gushes Sunset. "So is my friend Pinkie Pie!" She looks around, suddenly sad that her friend isn't here to share in the experience.

"Always great to meet a fan." K-Lo gives her a nod and twirls back into their VIP golf cart.

As they drive away, Sunset looks at the autograph. So cool! Not that she'll get to keep it.... By morning, the day will have reset, and it will be gone....

But when she wakes up the next morning and

reaches into her pocket...the autograph is *still there*.

"Huh? Weird."

Sunset hasn't been able to keep anything across the time loop until now. Not sure what to make of it, Sunset looks at her friends.

"Hey, guys, I kind of have a weird problem...."

The girls look at her in concern.

➡ GO TO PAGE 56.

SUNSET SHIMMER NEEDS SPACE.

"Particularly, to get out of the space you're in," Twilight Sparkle explains. Sunset nods, jotting down notes while Twilight elaborates, "By removing yourself from the point of space-time overlap, ie, the time loop, you'll shatter the day's spatial connection to time."

Sunset scribbles, trying to keep up with Twilight Sparkle's lightning-quick explanation. She sets down her pen and raises an eyebrow at Twilight, who sighs. "Too technical?" Sunset nods.

"Basically, you need to get as far away as you possibly can from the festival."

"That"—Sunset smiles—"I can do."

➡ GO TO PAGE 82.

SUNSET SHIMMER SHRUGS.

Why would she look a gift pony in the mouth? This whole repeating-day thing will probably work itself out. So as long as she's here she might as well have fun! But Starswirl has so much to offer. Where to start?

What should Sunset do?

➡ Relax to the max in the yoga yurts.
   GO TO PAGE 69.

➡ Beat the carnival games.
   GO TO PAGE 75.

➡ See. Every. Single. Band.
   GO TO PAGE 135.

"HEY, YOU'RE GONNA MESS UP MY HAIRDO!"

Sunset Shimmer snatches the Time Twirler out of K-Lo's hair. K-Lo grabs it, too, and they pull back and forth until it pops out of their hands.

K-Lo dives for it as it flies through the air, hits the ground, and shatters. K-Lo, Su-Z, and Sunset all stare at the broken pieces.

K-Lo sighs. "Are you happy with yourself? Now we can never deactivate the Time Twirler."

"We're stuck here...forever?"

Su-Z shrugs and eats a sushi kebab. "Welp, it's gonna be a long eternity."

The bandmates start bickering back and forth. Sunset can't believe she's stuck here forever with these two!

THE END

SUNSET SHIMMER BREATHES IN.

So she's stuck in a time loop because of ancient Equestrian magic. The last thing she needs to do is panic. And luckily for her, the latest trend in festival experiences is organized wellness. She breathes out.

The yoga yurt is an oasis of cool and calm in the middle of the hot festival grounds. Sunset feels the eucalyptus mist relaxing her with each breath. Pinkie Pie pops in at her side, taking a big whiff of the mist and coughing.

"You sure this is how you want to spend Starswirl, Sunset?"

Sandalwood, the yoga yurt's director, beckons to them. "Is life stressing you out? Come in and nama-*stay* as long as you like."

"Pinkie Pie, I'm definitely sure."

Sunset ditches Pinkie Pie and enters the crystal-shrined yurt. Sage burns, and weary festivalgoers roll out yoga mats. Sunset takes her place on a mat as Sandalwood leads them all in a yoga flow.

"Downward dog. Plank. Lunge. Hop to the front of your mat, and bow."

Sunset struggles to keep up, frustrated.

Sandalwood teaches, "This is what we call a sun salutation."

Sunset breaks her concentration, nudging the yogi to her right. "My name's Sunset, so I guess I'm more suited to sun farewells than sun salutations."

"The mind's chatter only disconnects us from ourselves." Sandalwood has opened one eye to judge Sunset. "Now, tree pose."

The entire class except Sunset moves as a unit, standing on one leg, palms touching peacefully, eyes closed. Sunset tries to follow suit, but she can't help looking around. Who knew standing still could be so much work!

What should Sunset do?

➡ Achieve enlightenment. **GO TO PAGE 48**.

➡ This isn't her thing. **GO BACK TO PAGE 67** to choose a different kind of festival fun!

"WHEN THE GOIN' GETS TOUGH, THE TOUGH GET...EVEN MORE TOUGH!"

Applejack straightens her hat and marches briskly toward the security guard. Feeling less confident, Sunset struggles to keep up.

"Shouldn't we make a plan or something, Applejack?"

"No use delayin' it."

"On second thought he's pretty big. Maybe we shouldn't give him a talking-to, tough or otherwise." Sunset digs her heels into the ground as Applejack pulls her forward. "What if he's mean?"

"We'll handle it."

"Wait!"

"Here we go!"

They're in front of the security guard now,

who stoically blows another bubble gum bubble. Applejack firmly pokes it. *Pop!*

"Don't mean to burst your bubble, but you gotta let us backstage." She leans right into his gum-coated face. "Or. Else."

The security guard takes off his sunglasses, glowering.

He scoffs. "Or else what?"

Applejack scoffs right back at him. "Or else you'll see."

"I don't think you know who you're messing with," he says.

"I don't think you know who you don't think knows who is messing with you," she fires back.

An awkward pause. Applejack steels herself and says in her most serious voice, "It's me."

Sunset shrinks behind Applejack, wincing. This isn't gonna be good.

The security guard blinks. Then he breaks out into a hearty laugh.

"You know what? You kids are all right—get on back there!"

Applejack grabs Sunset's hand, and they run past him before he changes his mind.

Sunset's mind is blown. "I can't believe that worked!"

Applejack shrugs. "We speak the same language. Now let's track down those no-good Dazzlings. Where could they be?"

Sunset notices a silvery tent with misters, buckets of refreshments, and sushi appetizers being passed around. It's the artists' backstage lounge. "Well, that seems like a good place to start."

➡ GO TO PAGE 38.

"THIS THING'S GOTTA BE RIGGED."

Applejack hurls yet another softball at a tower of milk bottles, but it just bounces off it. She grumbles as she eyes the elusive prize: a life-size Alicorn plushie.

Sunset Shimmer taps her on the shoulder. "Let me give it a whirl."

Sunset closes one eye, winds up a pitch, and throws. The milk bottles fall to the floor with a clatter.

Applejack's eyebrows rise up to the brim of her hat, impressed, as the booth worker hands the Alicorn plushie to Sunset.

"Hey, now, just what's your secret, Sunset? I've been tryin' all day to win."

Sunset shrugs coyly. "Practice, I guess."

"Wow-wow-kapow!" a voice exclaims. "That

is the freshest, sickest, most literally A-plus plushie I've ever seen!"

Sunset turns around to see none other than PostCrush!

What should Sunset do?

➡ Give the Alicorn to Applejack and choose a different kind of festival fun. **GO BACK TO PAGE 67**.

➡ Give the Alicorn to PostCrush. **GO TO PAGE 64**.

SCIENCE!

"It's just like magic, except with more numbers! So basically it's magic, but better," says Twilight Sparkle with a wink.

Sunset Shimmer's predicament is unfortunate, sure, but it's also a great time to test out some groundbreaking hypotheses. Who needs Starswirl Music Festival when you could *be* the next Star Swirl the Bearded? "Except with less beard," Sunset suggests. Twilight nods, hardly able to contain herself.

"We're dealing with space-time, which breaks down into two major factors: space. And time."

Sunset smirks. "You don't say."

But Twilight Sparkle explains that if they were able to break one of those two elements, it would definitely have an effect on the time loop.

"The only other potential possibility is..." Twilight trails off, lost in thought.

Sunset waves in front of her face. "Hello? Sunset to Twilight."

"Well, the only other idea is to disrupt the day's events so much that it isn't the same day anymore."

"What do you mean? Like going left instead of right? Wearing green instead of orange?" Somewhere, in the distance, Rarity shrieks at the thought.

Twilight Sparkle gulps. "More like getting the music festival canceled."

She continues. "Of course, there are limitless theories to test...but luckily we have all the time in the world! We could do experiment after experiment after experiment!" She chuckles before catching Sunset's glare. Twilight clears her throat.

"Er, sorry, this is a very serious situation that I want to help you find a very real solution to."

Sunset shakes her head, laughing now. "Just a little run-of-the-mill space-time disruption. But where to start?"

What should Sunset do?

➡ Disrupt time. **GO TO PAGE 40**.

➡ Disrupt space. **GO TO PAGE 66**.

➡ Disrupt the day's events.
   GO TO PAGE 138.

SUNSET SHIMMER VEERS LEFT.

It's a split-second decision. She grabs Rarity, and they head full speed down the path as it gets twistier and turnier. Then, suddenly, Sunset finds herself face-to-face with none other than...

...*herself.*

Sunset screams. Rarity peers over her shoulder and touches up Sunset's hair a little bit.

"There, there, darling, nothing a little comb can't fix."

Sunset looks around. Somehow they've found themselves in a hall of mirrors. Rarity gleefully applies lip gloss, primping and posing for a selfie. "What stylish company we've found ourselves among."

"Tee-hee-hee!"

A disembodied giggle echoes through the

halls. Sunset tries to follow it, but no matter where she goes, she always runs into herself.

"I think this is a dead end, Rarity. We'd better head back out."

But back-to-back, the girls look around, at a loss.

"All right, dear. Um, which way would that be?"

Sunset sighs. Guess they're stuck here for the night.

➡ **GO TO PAGE 102.**

SUNSET SHIMMER'S HANDS GRIP THE GLAMPING RV'S STEERING WHEEL.

The morning sun peeks over the horizon, gleaming across her sunglasses as she speeds down the highway. She smirks and pumps the gas, going faster.

"Sunset at sunrise."

She glances to the back of the cabin, where her friends are still sound asleep. Bummer they missed out on her awesome line. She clears her throat and says louder, *"Ahem!* Sunset...at sunrise!"

Pinkie Pie rouses, rubbing her eyes. "Are we... moving?"

The rest of the Mane Seven wake up, confused. Rainbow Dash stares out the back window, seeing Starswirl fade farther into the distance.

"Sunset, what are you doing? The first day of Starswirl is today!"

"You've gotta turn back!" Applejack cries. "We're running out of time to get ready!"

Sunset tilts down her sunglasses, gritting her teeth and punching the gas. "I'm not running out of time...I'm *out*running it!"

Rarity leaps into the passenger seat and buckles in.

"Darling, are you feeling quite all right?"

Pinkie Pie pops her head in. "And why are you acting all action-movie-star-y? I mean, I like it, but why?"

Bang! Just like that, the RV gets a flat tire and the girls are thrown into a jumble. After making sure everyone is okay, the girls pile out of the RV.

On the side of the road, Applejack examines the flat tire. "Well," she says as she tosses aside a nail, "there's your problem."

Sunset shrugs. "That's okay. I'll just try again tomorrow."

But the next day, she gets another flat. And another. And another. Weeks pass and Applejack emerges from under the RV with an array of obstacles: nails, scrap metal, a screwdriver. Sunset's lost her cool action-hero vibe. Her hair is frazzled.

One day, Applejack emerges yet again with a medieval mace. "No idea what this here mace was doing on the highway, but yep, that's a flat."

Sunset bursts into tears.

Her friends look to one another in concern. Pinkie Pie hugs her. "If you didn't want to go to Starswirl, you could've just told us."

Sunset wipes her eyes. She's tried everything she could think of. There's nothing for her to do except..."I give up."

How much time has passed? Weeks? Months? Sunset can't even bring herself to consider that a whole year has passed. The next morning, she watches glumly as her friends, yet again, get ready for the first day of Starswirl in the glamping RV.

Sunset mouths along as Pinkie Pie rants: "I can't believe Starswirl day one is already so much fun, even before we're inside the festival. Starswirl morning one for the win—wow, Sunset, you're mouthing along with me perfectly!"

Inside the festival, her friends split up and run joyfully in every direction while Sunset glumly walks the fairgrounds. So much for her perfect festival experience. She's seen PostCrush dozens of times; she's won every stuffed animal there is to win. For a while, she had fun freaking out Snips and Snails by predicting their every move, but even that lost its fun after a few days.

Puffed Pastry tries to tempt her with a free sample: "If you guess my secret ingredient, I'll give you free pastries for life!"

Without even trying it, Sunset replies, "Sunflower seeds."

Puffed Pastry blanches. "I mean, that wasn't a binding contract!"

Sunset walks on, sadly appraising the happy faces around her, unaware that they've lived this day a hundred times and in all likelihood will live it a hundred more. Sunset's resigned to her fate. To no one, she mutters, "You could spend eternity trying to make everything perfect, and it never would be."

"Deep," a voice agrees. Could this be the culprit behind the time loop? But then Sandalwood steps out of the shadows. "Kinda makes me think, like, this is the first day of the rest of our lives, you know?"

Sunset sighs. "I know better than you can possibly imagine."

THE END

SUNSET SHIMMER SHUTS HER EYES TIGHTLY AND DRIFTS OFF TO SLEEP.

What a weird dream. The best way to deal with nightmares is to sleep more, and that's exactly what Sunset does, counting Spikes as they fly over a picket fence. Slowly, she drifts off...

Until...

"SUNSET REGINALD SHIMMER!"

Sunset opens her eyes to see Pinkie Pie, who explains, "I know that isn't your middle name, but maybe it should be."

Looking around in confusion, Sunset sees the sun is high in the sky and flooding the RV with light.

"It's already lunchtime! You've slept all morning, but I didn't want to miss out on seeing PostCrush with you!"

Sunset gasps and sits upright. This is really happening. She really is repeating the day.

But what should she do next?

➡ Go see PostCrush. **GO TO PAGE 27**.

➡ Tell her friends that she needs help. **GO TO PAGE 56**.

*T*HUD.

Sunset Shimmer hits the ground.

SQUEAK.

Pinkie Pie hits the ground beside her.

The security guard slams the gate to the makeshift jail cell and rubs his jaw. "This is where we put troublemakers so they don't keep makin' trouble. So...don't keep makin' trouble."

"Us? Trouble? More like *treble*." Pinkie Pie leans over to their cellmates. "We're in a band—it's a music joke."

The girls sharing their cell look at each other. "Oh yeah," one of them says, "we're in a band called Wild Ones, ever heard of it? We're supposed to be playing tonight, but we lost our artist passes!"

Sunset rolls her eyes. She can't get out of there fast enough!

But as always, tomorrow is another day. Or rather, the same day...

Maybe next time she should try Rainbow Dash's plan or Applejack's approach to getting past this tough guy of a security guard.

———

What should Sunset do?

➡ Give this security guard a tough talking-to with Applejack. **GO TO PAGE 72.**

➡ Try to sneak past the security guard with Rainbow Dash. **GO TO PAGE 117.**

"IT'S MORNING!"

Pinkie Pie yells in Sunset Shimmer's face on yet another Starswirl day-one morning. Sunset's eyes blearily open and then...Sunset wraps Pinkie in a tight hug!

Pinkie coughs and confetti comes out. "Are you ready for a perfect day?"

Sunset smiles. "Yep."

Inside the festival walls, Pinkie Pie marvels, taking in Starswirl for the first time. Her excitement is infectious, and Sunset runs along with her as the confetti cannon fires.

"THERE'S A CONFETTI CANNON?!"

Just like the very, very first day, Pinkie asks, "What do you wanna do first, Sunset?"

Sunset smiles.

"What do *you* want to do, Pinkie Pie?"

Pinkie Pie lights up. "I'm so, so, so, so super glad you asked! I have a couple ideas, and I can't choose. There's a paint party that sounds pretty poppin'. But then there's the human pinball game! Or the food-truck tasting!"

Sunset shrugs. "Why choose? Let's do all three!" Pinkie's eyes go wide as Sunset grabs her hand with a wink. "You only live Starswirl once!"

Pinkie's stoked.

"All this and seeing PostCrush tonight with my best friend? Talk about a perfect day!"

➡ **GO TO PAGE 61.**

"**A** FASHION SHOW!"

Rarity whips out a rack of clothing from who knows where.

"The festival maze is—in a word—*amazing*." She nudges Sunset Shimmer. "Get it, darling? Anyhoo, it's exactly what I envisioned as a location for my summer lookbook."

She puts an arm around Sunset, pointing out the lush green canopy and vibrant neon. "It's technology meets tropical. Nature meets neon. Vacation meets business!"

"Well, I can't argue with that. Though I am a little confused about how you were able to casually lug around a week's worth of clothes."

Rarity puts a finger to Sunset's lips. "No time to explain! Couture is calling!"

Rarity twirls Sunset around, and suddenly Sunset is covered head to toe in sequins.

"Smile for the camera, darling!"

Just then, the mysterious stranger drops in on them from above.

"Did somebody say photoshoot?!"

She removes her feathered mask to reveal none other than—

"Trixie!" Sunset balks.

"Yes! It is I! The Great and Powerful Trixie! Though for Starswirl I have adopted a festival persona, and I wish to be referred to as...the Festival Fairy."

Trixie waves her arms, trying to be mysterious. Then she corrects herself, "Er, the Great and Powerful Festival Fairy!"

Sunset points at her accusatorily.

"You! You're the one behind all this. You somehow got ahold of the Time Twirler and are causing Starswirl day one to repeat!"

Trixie looks Sunset right in the eyes. "Am I great? Yes. Am I powerful? Yes. Do I have any idea what you're talking about? Not at all."

Before Sunset can process this, Rarity pushes them both out of the maze and onto a fashion runway. Snapgab influencers make up the audience, cheering and taking photos. Sunset works the runway, finding her inner fashion model. She gets to the end of the catwalk and strikes a pose. Cameras snap—*FLASH!*

That reminds her. She's not any closer to figuring out who's behind this whole mess, is she?

➡ GO TO PAGE 102.

SUNSET SHIMMER CAN'T BELIEVE IT.

She's at a backstage lounge party with Post-Crush. Breathing the same air as PostCrush. Nibbling the same appetizers as PostCrush.

K-Lo glances in her direction, and Sunset is so starstruck that she has to turn around. She does some quick breathing exercises, whispering to herself, "Get it together, Sunset, play it cool."

She steels herself and saunters over toward K-Lo and Su-Z as casually as possible. Unfortunately, when she gets there, she immediately stubs her toe on K-Lo's chaise lounge.

"Ow!"

K-Lo glances up at her, mildly confused. Sunset fights through the pain and seizes the opportunity, reaching out for a handshake.

"Hi, I'm Sunset Shimmer. Big fan of yours."

"Oh, uh...how nice." K-Lo takes her hand.

WHOOSH! Out of nowhere, Sunset's powers activate. She gets an empathy flash!

Images come streaming through her mind. K-Lo found the Time Twirler when she stumbled across a mysterious portal. The first night, their show was a disaster. K-Lo points an accusing finger at Su-Z, while Su-Z blames K-Lo. They accidentally activate the Time Twirler, and a purple pulse of magic emanates from it. *WHOOSH!*

Sunset gasps slightly as she snaps back to reality. K-Lo is gripping her hand tighter now. Sunset looks up to see that the Time Twirler has been styled into K-Lo's hair along with other assorted gems. Seeing Sunset's glance, the pop star's eyes narrow.

"What did you say your name was?" K-Lo asks in a whisper.

Su-Z chimes in, "Yeah, I've never seen you in the artists' lounge before today."

K-Lo elbows her and looks around wildly to

see if anyone heard. *"Shh!"* She turns back to Sunset Shimmer and gives her a once-over. "So. You're stuck in the time loop, too, huh?"

Sunset nods wildly. "Yes! And you don't know how *relieved* I am that you guys are in it, too. Maybe since you have the Time Twirler, together we can—"

But K-Lo cuts her off. "How about instead of crashing our little party, we make a deal instead? It just so happens that PostCrush is looking for a third member."

"Hey, I didn't know that!" objects Su-Z. K-Lo elbows her again and winks at Sunset.

"What do you say?"

***

What should Sunset do?

➡ Grab the Time Twirler and put an end to all this. **GO TO PAGE 68.**

➡ Join PostCrush! **GO TO PAGE 122.**

WHAT'S SUNSET SHIMMER WAITING FOR?

The clear culprits are right there, onstage, in front of her! The Dazzlings twirl as they sing their auto-tuned song.

"Need a leg up?" Pinkie Pie gives Sunset a boost, and suddenly she's crowd-surfing right toward the stage! Pinkie isn't far behind her. Sunset's boots hit the stage with a thud. Adagio Dazzle's jaw drops, and she lets out a gasp that even auto-tune can't mask. Their backing track warbles down to nothing.

"You!" Adagio growls.

"Me." Sunset smirks.

"Us!" yowls Pinkie Pie as the crowd tosses her onstage in a jumble.

Sunset helps Pinkie Pie up as Aria Blaze and Sonata Dusk take their places at Adagio's side.

Like an evil chorus, they say in unison, "What are *you* doing here?"

Sunset lunges toward them. "The Time Twirler—where is it?!"

Sonata Dusk steps forward into the spotlight and shakes the hair from her eyes. "We," she says, "have no idea what you're talking about."

"A Time Twirly? What is it, like a watch?" asks Aria Blaze.

There's an awkward silence. The microphone screeches feedback. Pinkie Pie leans over to Sunset. "Yeah, what is it exactly?"

Sunset is crestfallen, but she sets her face into a grimace to hide her disappointment. So the Dazzlings are here, but they have nothing to do with the time loop?

"Booooo!"

Sunset turns around—she totally forgot about the crowd! And they aren't happy. A tomato hits her square in the nose. Sunset throws her arms up, exasperated.

"Okay, who brings tomatoes to a music festival?"

Adagio cuts the power to the instruments and motions for the security guard. "Get them out of here."

Sunset looks over to see the stocky security guard stalking their way. Pinkie Pie leans over and gulps. "Uh, I think he means business."

What should Sunset do?

➡ Run. **GO TO PAGE**...Let's be honest,
there's nowhere to run. **GO TO PAGE 89**.

"I AM *NOT* IN THE MOOD FOR THIS!"

Sunset Shimmer has just woken up on the first day of Starswirl. Yet again. She groans, to Pinkie Pie's befuddlement.

"What's the matter, Sunset? I thought we were gonna have a perfect day today."

Sunset sighs. "So did I."

Here she is again, back at the beginning. She doesn't even bother explaining it to Pinkie Pie. If she wasn't already frustrated, now she's just plain fed up.

Pinkie Pie sulks away. Twilight Sparkle notices Sunset's chagrin and comes over to her.

"What's going on, Sunset?"

Sunset glumly looks to Twilight. "To put it simply? I'm caught in a space-time loop."

Twilight brightens. "Oh, is that it? Well, have you tried breaking it?"

Sunset shrugs. She's lost all hope. She's not sure she has much left to do except run away from her problems.

What should Sunset do?

➡ Try to break the time loop with Twilight Sparkle's help. **GO TO PAGE 77**.

➡ Run for the hills. **GO TO PAGE 82**.

"EVERYBODY COULD USE MORE FRIENDS!"

Pinkie Pie is sure of it.

"Even mean-looking tough-guy security guards?" asks Sunset Shimmer.

"Especially them!"

If anyone can win over this guy, it's Pinkie Pie. Sunset decides it's worth a shot.

"When the going gets tough—" begins Sunset.

"We ask nicely!" finishes Pinkie.

Sunset and Pinkie approach the security guard, who stoically watches them get closer. He has no reaction whatsoever to them, even when they're right in front of him. They look back at themselves in his mirrored sunglasses. It's as if he's staring through them! Sunset gulps as Pinkie jumps in front of him.

"Hi, mister! How are you?"

He doesn't reply.

"Enjoying the music? Or is this really more of a job for you? What are your interests?"

He doesn't reply.

"Favorite color?"

He doesn't reply.

Pinkie looks to Sunset Shimmer, who shrugs. Pinkie clears her throat.

"Well, now that we're old friends, we have a favor to ask you. See, it's a long story, but there are people back there who are definitely up to no good, and we need to figure out what they're doing. Would you please kindly, oh-so-nicely let us back there for just a little bit?"

To Sunset's shock, a big smile cracks across the security guard's face and he says, "Why of course!"

Even Pinkie Pie is surprised, stuttering, "R-really?"

The security guard's face falls.

"No."

He gruffly takes each of them by an elbow.

"You're not goin' backstage, but I can take you to another exclusive area of the festival...."

Pinkie and Sunset lock eyes. This can't be good.

⟶ **GO TO PAGE 89.**

"*IT'S MORNING!*"

Like every other day, Sunset Shimmer opens her eyes to find Pinkie Pie's inches away. It can't be. They deactivated the Time Twirler!

"Specifically, morning on Starswirl day two!"

Sunset lets out a sigh of relief and starts laughing. Her friends are all around her, excited to share the day with her.

"What do you wanna do today, Sunset?" Pinkie Pie asks brightly.

Sunset smiles. "I'm done choosing. Someone else decide!"

They pile out of the glamping RV and head for the festival, chattering excitedly about all of the day's scheduled events. There's music echoing through the trees, balloons flying, and the smell of fresh-baked pastries wafting from food trucks. Sunset breathes in the fresh forest air as if she's doing it for the first time.

THE END

THE RAINBOOMS HAVE NEVER HAD
FANS LIKE THIS.

Sunset Shimmer signs a loopy autograph for a fan who's sobbing with joy. Rainbow Dash poses for a photo with a few giddy kids. A familiar voice pipes up:

"Can I puh-lease, pretty please with sprinkles have your autograph?"

It's Pinkie Pie! Sunset gives her a hug, and Pinkie Pie is shocked, not recognizing Sunset under all her stage makeup and the outlandish outfit.

"Pinkie Pie, it's me!" Sunset winks.

"I know, you're in Wild Ones!"

"No, I mean, you and I are really *friends*!"

Pinkie is so moved by this that she gets a little weepy. "I humbly accept the title of *friend* and hope that I can one day live up to it!"

Sunset laughs, assuring her, "Hey, you *are* a great friend! You already live up to that title." Sunset signs an autograph for her, and Pinkie beams.

"Thank you so much!"

Pinkie zigzags away, delighted. As Sunset watches her go, she can't help feeling a little guilty. Pinkie Pie has always been an amazing friend. It was Sunset who wasn't such a great friend on the very first Starswirl day one. She regrets yelling at Pinkie, but there's no time to dwell on that! Her public demands her.

"Over here!" Someone shakes her hand.

She and Rainbow Dash stand back-to-back and people snap photos with their phones. Rainbow Dash leans over and whispers, "Doesn't get any better than this."

Then a guy in a red tank top checks the picture he just took. "Hey! You aren't in Wild Ones! You're imposters!"

Whoops.

Sunset and Rainbow Dash make a break for it, but they run directly into the security guard, who looms over them and snorts.

"You girls just got yourselves banned from Starswirl. For life."

➡ **GO TO PAGE 102.**

"**P**LAY IT COOL, PLAY IT COOL, PLAY IT COOL,**"** Pinkie chants as she and Sunset Shimmer walk up to PostCrush. But as soon as they're there, she bursts out, "HI I'M PINKIE PIE AND THIS IS MY FRIEND SUNSET AND WE LOVE YOU SO, SO MUCH!"

Sunset laughs and reaches out for a handshake. Su-Z stares at them, blankly suspicious.

"But you guys weren't here on any of the other days—"

K-Lo elbows her, says, *"Shh!"*, and turns to Sunset, offering her hand.

"Always fantastic to meet a fan!"

Pinkie Pie shakes her hand vigorously, but Sunset can tell something's up. She reaches out and takes K-Lo's hand.

WHOOSH. Empathy flash.

Images come streaming through her mind. K-Lo found the Time Twirler when she stumbled across a mysterious portal. The first night, their show was a disaster. K-Lo points an accusing finger at Su-Z, while Su-Z blames K-Lo. They accidentally activate the Time Twirler, and a purple pulse of magic emanates from it.

Sunset gasps slightly as she snaps back to reality. K-Lo is gripping her hand tighter now. Sunset looks up to see that the Time Twirler has been styled into K-Lo's hair along with other assorted gems. Seeing Sunset's glance, the pop star's eyes narrow.

"What did you say your name was?" K-Lo asks in a whisper.

Sunset reels back. "It's *you*! You're the ones using the Time Twirler!"

"You're right." K-Lo smirks, pacing now. "But I wouldn't expect you to understand.

Starswirl is our big reunion show. Our last moment in the spotlight. It must. Be. *Perfect*."

Su-Z rolls her eyes. "Well, maybe if you learned your choreography."

"Well, maybe if you could hit the high notes!" K-Lo claps back.

Sunset's horrified. Pinkie Pie leans over to whisper, "This doesn't seem like a great time, but what's going on?"

"*Security!*" Su-Z screeches. "There, K-Lo. How's that for a high note?"

The security guard throws Pinkie Pie and Sunset into PostCrush's tour bus and locks the door. Pinkie looks around, wide-eyed.

"I can't believe we're in PostCrush's real-life tour bus! And also that they're evil! What's that Time Twirler thing you were talking about?"

Sunset sighs. Where to start?

"This all started when I was a bad friend to you. I wanted a perfect day, but I only cared about having it *my* way. So when I got a chance to have a do-over, I thought it was because of my wish."

Pinkie Pie listens somberly. Sunset explains about the repetitive days and how she wasn't ever able to figure it out.

"But did you ever have a perfect day?" Pinkie asks.

Sunset smiles.

"Not until today. Because I spent it with you."

"Really? Even though our heroes locked us in their tour bus and will probably keep this day repeating forever?"

Sunset nods.

"Even after that."

They hear the distant roar of a crowd. PostCrush is about to go onstage.

"How many days do you think you've been here?" Pinkie asks.

Sunset considers and then laughs. "Let's just say, happy birthday."

Pinkie's beside herself. "It's my birthday?!" Ecstatic, she pulls out pastries she saved from the lounge and starts bursting them into confetti. *Pop! Pop! Pop!* Between gleeful confetti bursts, she says very seriously, "But also that's horrible you've spent so long in this time loop, I'm so sorry. But also happy birthday to *meeee*!"

Sunset laughs as Pinkie pulls out a particularly hefty cupcake and bursts it into confetti—

BLAM!

The confetti blasts the tour bus door open. Sunset looks to Pinkie.

"Did you even mean to do that?"

"Nope. Now let's go save the day!"

➡ **GO TO PAGE 131.**

"WE'LL BE BACKSTAGE IN A FLASH."

Rainbow Dash watches the security guard, waiting for the perfect moment when his head's turned.

"Here, hop on my back, Sunset!"

Sunset Shimmer does, and *zip!* They're off! Rainbow Dash uses her super speed to give Sunset a piggyback ride at the speed of a cheetah-back ride. They whizz past the security guard while he's preoccupied with picking a particularly tough booger.

He feels the breeze as they pass and looks up, embarrassed to be caught picking his nose. But when he sees that he's still alone, he smirks, smugly thinking he got away with it, when it's actually Sunset who pulled off the caper.

Backstage, Sunset hops off Rainbow Dash's back, and they high-five.

"It worked!"

"Duh, it worked. Super speed always works."

"Now we just have to confront the Dazzlings, get the Time Twirler, and break the time loop! Easy!"

Suddenly, a hand grabs each of their shoulders. Uh-oh. The security guard must have caught them after all.

"Maybe not so easy," whispers Rainbow Dash.

"There you are!"

It's not the security guard at all. It's a frazzled event organizer. He speaks into his walkie-talkie.

"Copy that, found the missing members of Wild Ones. Bringing them to hair and makeup now." He leads them into the hair-and-makeup tent. "You artistic types. Always wandering off when you're supposed to be onstage!"

Sunset and Rainbow Dash lock eyes with each other. Onstage? Rainbow Dash is about to protest when Sunset elbows her. Might as well go along with this!

Suddenly, they're in a flurry of assistants who pat them with makeup, spray them with hairspray, and pile chiffon stage outfits onto them. Sunset coughs through a cloud of glitter, and when it clears...

The audience is cheering.

Sunset and Rainbow Dash are onstage in front of a wild crowd, wielding keytars. They exchange a frantic glance. Their confused bandmates look at them—they're not who they were expecting. But then Sunset nods.

"Let's rock."

They start playing, and Sunset and Rainbow Dash find their groove. Stage lights flash as Rainbow Dash wails on her keytar, delivering an insane solo. The crowd goes wild as Sunset joins her, back-to-back.

Their impromptu bandmates smile and

egg them on, impressed. As they finish their set, fans throw flower crowns and streamers onstage—the crowd loves them! They take their bows and head offstage, clapping one another on the back.

"Great show, Wild Ones!"

As Rainbow Dash takes off her keytar, a slick-looking rock star comes her way.

"Saw your show—that's the fastest playing I've ever seen! Sorry, I shoulda introduced myself, I'm—"

Rainbow Dash gasps. "Riff Slider! You're Deviant Septum's guitarist."

"The one and only."

Rainbow Dash's jaw is on the floor. Her hero just acknowledged her. She turns to Sunset. "Best. Day. Ever!"

Riff nods toward a silvery tent that emanates coolness. "So, where ya headed? To the artists' lounge?"

A group of fans break backstage, encircling

them and asking for autographs. Sunset and Rainbow Dash share a smile—they're rock stars!

What should Sunset do?

➡ Chill out in the artists' lounge.
GO TO PAGE 38.

➡ Hang with the fans. **GO TO PAGE 109**.

SUNSET SHIMMER IS OFFICIALLY A MEMBER OF THE POP DUO POSTCRUSH!

"I guess that technically makes us a pop trio, right? So cool!" Sunset is ecstatic. It's a dream come true as she gets ready in their tour bus. K-Lo wears all gold, while Su-Z wears all silver, and Sunset dons all bronze.

K-Lo smirks. "Ready for your first show? Just follow my lead and you'll do fine."

As they approach the stage from the wings, Sunset hears the crowd cheering. It's surreal as they step out into the spotlight. The audience roars, snapping pictures. This is next level. Sunset hasn't just met her heroes; she has become one of them.

The music starts, and she sings and dances her heart out.

She leans over the stage, reaching out to the screaming fans, who reach back to touch her hand. Pinkie Pie is among them, looking confused but impressed.

A twang of guilt hits Sunset, wishing she could share this with her bestie.

"Sunset, back to position!" K-Lo whisper-yells.

Sunset falls into line with the other two, and they dance across the stage, kicking and ducking under one another's legs. Confetti shoots out from the stage for their final number, and the three of them take a bow.

As they head offstage, Sunset's aglow with adrenaline. "You guys do this every night? That was amazing!"

K-Lo shrugs, unimpressed. "It was okay. Su-Z's voice was flat on that last note."

Su-Z reels. "Well, your dancing was sloppy at best."

Sunset's taken aback by their negativity. "I thought it was perfect."

They turn to her in unison. "Don't get me started on you."

Sunset's perturbed. "So you're just going to repeat the day until you have a perfect performance?"

"That's the idea," says Su-Z.

K-Lo pats Sunset on the back. "Look, you've had a nice day, but why don't you get some rest. We have another performance tomorrow."

Su-Z pulls out her instant-film camera and snaps a picture of Sunset.

"Just a little something to commemorate your first show with us!"

Sunset goes back to the glamping RV, feeling happier than she has in...well...days! Maybe being stuck in a time loop isn't such a bad thing—it helped her become a part of her favorite band!

The next morning, Sunset hurries out of bed before the rest of her friends and makes her way to PostCrush's tour bus. She walks up to the security guard.

"Hi! PostCrush is expecting me."

To her surprise, the guard pulls the instant film photo that Su-Z took out of his pocket and compares it to Sunset.

"They sure are. Come with me." The security guard grabs Sunset's shoulder.

"Oof!" Sunset hits the dirt outside the festival.

The security guard brushes off his hands. "No crazy fan is getting in on my watch."

K-Lo and Su-Z appear over his shoulder and smile nastily.

"Not just anybody can be in PostCrush. So you better get used to being thrown out of PostCrush every day for the rest of forever," Su-Z sneers.

Sunset is crestfallen. She had her chance, and she blew it. PostCrush will never let her near them again.

"Sometimes," K-Lo says with a laugh, "you just don't get a do-over."

THE END

"**W**HO WAS SPYING ON US?"

"And why were they laughing all mysteriously?" Pinkie Pie wonders aloud.

"That was the knowingest laugh I ever heard," says Applejack.

"Such a mysterious and trendy silhouette!" agrees Rarity.

Rainbow Dash points after the stranger. "Follow that trend!"

Sunset sprints across the fairgrounds, leaping over sunbathing concertgoers, ducking under Zephyr Breeze's hacky sack game. She slides over a runaway churro cart as if she's the star of an action movie and it's the hood of a car. She squints in the sunlight.

"There! By the neon garden maze!"

Sunset looks over her shoulder to see that

the churro cart has left everyone in a jumble. Well, almost everyone. Rarity grabs her hand.

"The show must go on, darling!"

The two of them race to the neon garden maze, hot on the heels of the unknown chuckler. Just as Sunset turns each corner, she barely catches a glimmer of the person as they turn the next. Sunset and Rarity are full speed ahead, when—*THWACK*—the path splits and they run right into the wall.

"Which way did they go?"

Rarity shrugs. "I haven't the faintest clue!"

What should Sunset do?

➡ Go right. **GO TO PAGE 32**.

➡ Go left. **GO TO PAGE 80**.

➡ Have a fashion show. Wait, what?
   GO TO PAGE 93.

*T*HE SECURITY GUARD CHEWS GUM
DISINTERESTEDLY, BLOWING A MEN-
ACING BUBBLE.

Sunset Shimmer narrows her eyes as his
bubble pops. He's the only thing standing between her and getting to the bottom of what's
going on here. But Fluttershy's right. They're
not Very Important People, so they can't just
walk into where all the actually important
people are. What they need is a different solution. Sunset thinks out loud, "We don't have
backstage passes, so getting backstage is gonna
require some—"

"Friendship?" suggests Pinkie Pie.

"High-speed maneuvering," Rainbow Dash
offers.

Applejack cracks her knuckles. "You can
always fight tough with tough."

What should Sunset do?

➡ Toughen up with Applejack.
   GO TO PAGE 72.

➡ Befriend the security guard with
   Pinkie Pie. **GO TO PAGE 104.**

➡ Sneak past the security guard with
   Rainbow Dash. **GO TO PAGE 117.**

SUNSET SHIMMER AND PINKIE PIE RUN AS FAST AS THEY CAN.

On the main stage, PostCrush greets their fans. As they start to play their first song, Pinkie Pie and Sunset crash the stage. The crowd gasps.

K-Lo is taken aback."What?! How?!"

"Pastries!" Pinkie Pie yells triumphantly.

Sunset snatches the Time Twirler out of K-Lo's elaborate hairdo.

Su-Z falls to her knees.

"Don't! Please!"

Sunset shrugs. "Nothing's perfect."

And with that, she deactivates the Time Twirler. K-Lo fumes.

"You ruined our perfect reunion show! I really had a good feeling about this one!"

Sunset gestures to the audience. Their fans wait, holding their collective breath.

"They don't want perfection. Your fans just want *you*. The real you, flaws and all. Rocking out and having fun with each other."

Su-Z looks to K-Lo. "It *has* been a while since we had fun doing this. Like we used to, when we started."

K-Lo nods. "We used to be friends. Now we're just...bandmates."

"Who cares if you put on a perfect show? Life's about the messes you make along the way."

"And the people you make them with!"

Pinkie Pie pops up next to her with a poof of cupcake confetti.

"So what do you say? One more song."

Sunset leads the crowd in chanting, "One more song! One more song!"

K-Lo and Su-Z look out at their fans,

moved. And then to each other. Su-Z helps K-Lo to her feet.

"Let's crush it," K-Lo says with a grin.

The crowd goes wild. Su-Z tosses drum sticks to Pinkie Pie, and K-Lo tosses a guitar to Sunset Shimmer.

"We could use some backup. If you want."

And just like that, Pinkie Pie and Sunset Shimmer are actually playing Starswirl with their favorite band. K-Lo lets herself dance as wildly as she wants, and Su-Z improvises a new verse. Fans lose their minds, loving it.

In the audience, Rainbow Dash, Twilight Sparkle, Rarity, Applejack, and Fluttershy all look up quizzically at the stage.

"I don't know why they're onstage, exactly..." says Fluttershy.

"But it is *awesome*!" finishes Rainbow Dash.

They start dancing, cheering on their friends.

Pinkie Pie drums her heart out while Sunset

Shimmer wails on the guitar. They share a smile. A perfect ending to a perfect day.

➡ **GO TO PAGE 107.**

WHY CHOOSE?

With so many bands playing Starswirl, there's no way anyone could see all of them. Unless, of course, your name is Sunset Shimmer and you're stuck in a time loop caused by ancient Equestrian magic.

Even the least known band is sure to be huge a year from now. She's seen a DJ remix classical music into an insane dance beat. She's sung along to a new indie songwriter's acoustic jam. She's seen every act from hip-hop to country to alternative to hip-hop–country–alternative. Sunset's worked her way through the lineup, and now she's bobbing her head along at the goth-metal show. Not exactly her cup of tea, but it's definitely a look.

"Sunset?" a meek voice asks from behind her.

She turns around to see...

"Fluttershy?!"

Fluttershy is decked out with black eyeliner and a spike-chain bracelet. She replies cheerily, "Great to see you here! I didn't know you were a fan of Skullcrusher! Rock on!"

Fluttershy headbangs furiously. Sunset can't help laughing in surprise.

Sunset crosses Skullcrusher off her list. Soon she will have seen all the bands at Starswirl!

The next day, Sunset wanders around the festival grounds with her friends and mentally plans her band lineup for the day, when she hears lyrics drifting over the crowd:

"Every day is the same,
the same, the same.
Over and over again,
again, again..."

Sunset's eyes widen. Those lyrics can't just be a coincidence...can they?

***

What should Sunset do?

➡ Investigate the lyrics. This is beyond suspicious. **GO TO PAGE 34**.

➡ The lyrics probably mean nothing. Why bother checking? **GO BACK TO PAGE 67** to choose a different kind of festival fun.

Starswirl won't know what hit it.

"Your mission, should you choose to accept it..." Twilight Sparkle paces in front of Sunset Shimmer like a military general. Sunset raises her hand.

"I'll accept it. I really don't have much of a choice."

"Great. Then your objective is as follows: Get the music festival canceled."

Sunset thinks.

Later that day, the festival organizer is stressed. How can everything be going so wrong? First the food trucks mysteriously didn't receive their produce shipments, then the band

Deviant Septum had to cancel because they supposedly got a better gig, two members of the band Wild Ones never made it to sound check, and as if that wasn't enough, all the Starswirl merchandise has gone missing!

He paces back and forth, shouting into a walkie-talkie, completely oblivious to Sunset. She cartwheels back and forth like a stealthy ninja.

When he turns around, she freezes behind a perfectly arranged stack of boxes, holding an extension cord. Everything's going according to plan.

He sighs. "What else could go wrong?"

She pulls the plug, and all the lights go out.

A voice buzzes over his walkie-talkie. "Sir, the power just went out."

The organizer sighs for a long time. "Yes, I noticed that. This is the last straw. Starswirl is *canceled*!"

"Woo-hoo!" Sunset can't help but let out a cheer. The event organizer peers behind the boxes and sees her. She gulps. Then— *WHOOSH!* A purple light splits the sky, and suddenly it's morning again. She did it! But before Sunset can celebrate, the sun rises again. And again. And again. The day is still repeating, except now it's on fast-forward! Sunset walks through the festival, bewildered, as it blurs around her. The crowds rush by, moving at super speed. Bands play for an instant, then are done. What has she done?

Sunset sighs. Turns out, ripping the fabric of space-time can have some unintended consequences. Hypothesis: tested. Mission: failed.

THE END